# Warwickshire County Council

| | | |
|---|---|---|
| WMU 10/2| | **J** |
| KTN 04/23 | 0 5 JAN 2022 | |
| 0 2 SEP 2023 | 2 8 MAR 2022 | |
| | 1 2 APR 2022 | |
| 0 4 JUN 2022 | | |
| 1 7 OCT 2022 | | |
| 9 DEC 2023 | | |

KT-443-946

This item is to be returned or renewed before the latest date above. It may be borrowed for a further period if not in demand. **To renew your books:**

- **Phone the 24/7 Renewal Line 01926 499273 or**
- **Visit www.warwickshire.gov.uk/libraries**

  **Discover ● Imagine● Learn ● *with libraries***

**Warwickshire County Council**

Working for Warwickshire

Published by Sweet Cherry Publishing Limited
Unit 36, Vulcan House,
Vulcan Road,
Leicester, LE5 3EF
United Kingdom

First published in the UK in 2021
2021 edition

2 4 6 8 10 9 7 5 3 1

ISBN: 978-1-78226-930-4

Magic Animal Café: Herriot the Caretaker Mouse

Cover design by Fabiana Attanasio and Jessica Walters
Illustrations by Fabiana Attanasio

www.sweetcherrypublishing.com

Printed and bound in the United Kingdom
E.C007

# Magic Animal Café
## Herriot
### the Caretaker
### Mouse

Stella Tarakson

Illustrated by
Fabiana Attanasio

Sweet
Cherry

# Chapter One

'Can you get Mozart off the piano, love?'

Ellie tore her gaze from her sketch pad. 'Hmm?'

'Mozart,' Mum repeated. 'He's making an awful racket, and I'm trying to concentrate.' Bracelets jingling, she kneaded her forehead with one hand and leafed through a stack of papers with the other.

'All right.' Ellie put down her pencil on the packing crate that served as a temporary desk. She'd been too absorbed in her drawing to notice the tuneless *plink plonk plink*ing until now. She stood up and walked over to the piano. 'Come on, you.'

Ellie placed an arm under Mozart's fluffy belly and scooped him gently off the keys. He squirmed in protest, but settled on Ellie's lap when she sat cross-legged back on the floor. He placed a paw on Ellie's drawing.

'Do you miss it too?' she whispered into the cat's ear, so that her mum couldn't hear.

The house in Ellie's drawing was small and neat, with lace curtains and flowers in the window. It looked bright, cheerful and welcoming – not like the dump they lived in now, she thought.

Ellie and her mum had moved into the crumbling old building last week. They lived in one of two upstairs flats, where the ceilings were low, the windows were small, and the floorboards were dark and uneven. As unsettling as their flat was, however, it was nothing compared to what was downstairs.

The ground floor had been left empty for years. Before that, it had been used for all sorts of things, from a post office to a vet's surgery. Remains of these past lives

kept turning up in odd nooks and crannies: safety caps for medicine bottles, curled up scraps of paper, broken pens and pencils. Junk.

Just yesterday, Mum had discovered a peeling leather trunk covered with moth-eaten blankets. The trunk was fastened with a padlock and stashed in the bottom of an old cupboard. It looked mysterious, locked up and hidden away like that. Ellie couldn't help wondering what was inside – but it was probably only more rubbish, she decided.

'I'll deal with that later,' Mum had said, closing the cupboard door. 'After the electrician's gone.'

Ellie had to admit the place looked better since the electrician had put in new lights. Old newspaper still lined the street-facing window, but the place wasn't quite so gloomy, and the shadows weren't so deep. Still, there was a long way to go before it would be ready for customers. The painters and decorators were due soon, and there was so much left to do that her mum had quickly forgotten about the trunk.

'Ow!' Ellie yelped as Beethoven pounced on her, digging a claw into her thigh. Mozart yowled at the interruption, and the two cats started hissing and batting each other with their paws. Chopin stalked over to see what was going on.

'Stop it, you lot,' Mum said, waving a sheet of paper in their direction. 'I've got to order the sign this afternoon or it won't be ready for opening day, and I'm still not even sure about the name! What do you think, Ellie?'

'I thought you'd already decided.'

Mum had been agonising over what to call her new business for weeks:

Catmosphere, Purrfection, The Pawsome Café, The Clawsome Café.

'Yeah, but I think I've changed my mind again ...'

'Don't,' Ellie said. 'Cattucino's good. You should just pick something and go with it.'

'I suppose so.' Mum twisted one of her long dark curls through her fingers and smiled. 'You're so sensible. Maybe you should be running the cat café instead of me.'

Ellie opened her mouth to speak but thought better of it. It was true, her mum wasn't very businesslike. She was the artistic type, with her long flowing

dresses and armloads of bracelets.
Before the divorce, Mum had
been a concert pianist, and after

it a piano teacher
so that she could
spend more
time at home.
A few months
ago, she'd
inherited an old
building from
her grandfather
– Ellie's great-
grandfather –
and decided
to set up her
own business.

'It's the chance I've been looking for,' Mum had said, her eyes shining as she outlined her plans. 'We'll live on the first floor and rent out the second floor flat for extra money. You can help out in the café. It'll be great, sweetie, you'll see.'

Ellie hadn't wanted to move. She hadn't wanted to leave her friends or change schools or be forced to share their home with strangers.

'What time did you say that family is moving in?' Ellie asked.

'The Andersons? I'm not sure. Soon. You can give their son a tour.'

Even though she'd never met the Andersons, Mum expected Ellie to

make friends with their son simply because they were the same age. Ellie knew nothing about him! What if he was mean or spoilt or both? What if he was just boring?

Ellie heard the rumble of a van pull up outside. She swallowed nervously. 'They're here.'

# Chapter Two

Ellie and her mum stood in the narrow back lane as the removal men started to unload the van.

'Where do you want these?' a man in overalls asked, balancing two boxes.

'This way,' Mum said, beckoning him towards the rear entrance that led up to the flats. 'Ellie, wait here

for the Andersons while I show the men upstairs.'

As soon as Mum has gone, a car pulled up behind the removal van. The driver's door opened, and a man with deeply tanned skin climbed out. Shading his eyes, he looked up at the old stone building.

'We're here, Jen,' he said. 'Looks good, doesn't it?'

A woman stepped out of the car. She had sun-bleached hair and sky-blue eyes. She broke into a big smile. 'It's so old! There's nothing like this back home.'

The woman said 'old' like it was a *good* thing, thought Ellie. Couldn't

they see what a wreck this place was?

'Blake, come on out,' Mrs Anderson continued. 'This is our new home.'

Ellie watched silently as the rear passenger door opened. A skinny boy about her height leapt onto the footpath, dressed in a plain white T-shirt and jeans. He had shaggy hair the colour of wet sand. It flopped over his eyes, which were the same clear blue as his mum's.

'Cool,' he said, pushing the hair off his face.

'You hang on to Choccy while we direct the removalists.'

'Sure.'

Choccy? Who or what was a Choccy?

Mrs Anderson noticed Ellie for the first time. 'You must be Ellie! Hi, we're your new tenants. Is your mother here?'

'Yes, she's–'

'Hello, welcome!' Ellie's mum bustled towards them, her long dress floating behind her. 'I'm Susan. Nice to finally meet you.' The three adults shook hands, then hurried off to help the removal men.

Ellie was left alone with the boy. She eyed him uncertainly.

'G'day,' he said, stepping towards her and holding out his hand. 'I'm Blake.'

'Ellie.' Instead of shaking his hand – which seemed too weird – Ellie gave a stiff little wave.

Blake dropped his hand with a grin. He didn't seem at all put off. 'Nice to meetcha.'

'You too. Err ... you're welcome.' Ellie felt awkward and wasn't sure what to say.

'Thanks! It's great to be here – a bit cold, but Mum says we'll soon get used to it.'

'Where are you from?' Ellie asked, the boy's friendliness making her a bit less shy.

'Australia. We moved a few weeks ago. Mum and Dad are setting up an animal rescue centre. That's what they did back home. It's really cool.'

'I see.' That did sound kind of cool. 'Did you ever help them?'

'Heaps of times. It was mostly people's pets, but sometimes we saved wild animals too, like koalas and kangaroos – especially after a bushfire.'

'Wow,' Ellie breathed. She would love to nurse a cuddly baby koala!

They looked so adorable. 'So what's a choccy, then?' Maybe they'd already rescued some exotic animal and it was with them right now. Ellie tried to look past the boy to see into the car.

'A what?' Blake looked puzzled.

'Your mum said for you to hang on to the choccy.'

'Oh!' The boy's face cleared, and he laughed. 'Choccy's short for chocolate. We've got a Labrador.'

'You've got a what?!' Ellie couldn't believe her ears. Then Blake stepped aside, unblocking her view of the car. A dark brown puppy was standing on its hind legs on the

back seat with its face pressed to the window. Its mouth was open, showing pointy white teeth and a slobbering pink tongue.

'You can't have a dog!' Ellie cried.

Blake's good-natured face hardened slightly. 'Why not?'

'Because we have cats! *Lots* of them. We're opening a cat café!'

'I know that! There's nothing to worry about. Choccy's good as gold.'

Ellie folded her arms and looked doubtful. 'Are you sure?'

'Sure, I'm sure. Look, I'll get him out. Don't worry,' Blake said, as if guessing what Ellie would say next, 'he's on a lead.'

24

'Well, I don't know–' Ellie started, just as Blake wrenched open the car door. The puppy hurled itself at him. It jumped up and down in a frenzy of excitement, making high-pitched yipping noises.

'Sit, Choccy, sit,' Blake said uselessly, trying to press the dog's wriggling rump to the ground. Whenever he touched the dog's body, it twisted around, licked his hand, then kept on bouncing. 'He's not normally like this, I promise. He's just excited after the long drive.'

'Grab his lead!'

Ellie's warning came too late. Something must have caught the

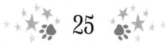

puppy's attention, because he
suddenly bolted – straight towards
the building's back door.

# Chapter Three

Ellie and Blake darted after the puppy. Blake lunged for the lead, which was trailing on the ground behind Choccy. He missed.

'Get him!' Ellie cried.

'I'm trying!' Blake made another grab, but it was too late. The Labrador puppy burst through the back room and into the still-unfurnished cat café,

tongue flapping and tail wagging.

It was as if a hurricane swept through the room. A flurry of cats seemed to turn in mid-air. Two jumped onto the piano, a few onto the counter, and the rest darted away. Unsure which cat to chase first, Choccy stood in the middle of the café and barked.

'Crikey, how many cats have you *got*?' Blake asked, finally catching up with his pet. He scooped him off the floor and held him tightly.

'Only eight.'

'*Only?*'

Ellie glared at the boy and his dog. 'You need lots of cats for a cat café.'

'I guess.' As Blake spoke, Choccy twisted around and licked him wetly on the face.

Ellie shuddered. Dogs were gross.

'See, he's calm now,' Blake said, wiping off the drool. 'He'll get used to the cats, you'll see. Everything will be fine.'

'Hmm.' Ellie wasn't convinced. Mozart was still clinging to the piano lid, his fur standing on end. Ellie had never seen him look so stressed before. Mozart was the oldest of all the cats, older than nine-year-old Ellie herself, and her clear favourite. She picked him up and clutched him to her chest.

'What are their names?' Blake asked, looking from one cat to another.

Ellie didn't feel like being nice, but she knew that Mum would be upset if she was rude. 'This is Mozart,' she said reluctantly. 'That's Beethoven. Those are Chopin, Handel and Grieg. Bach, Haydn and Vivaldi ran out.'

'So, they're all named after, erm-'

'Composers,' Ellie finished for him. 'Yes.'

'Cool. And the piano - do you play?'

'I try not to.' Ellie grimaced. 'Mum's making me learn, though. She's a musician.'

'That's awesome,' Blake said, looking at the piano wistfully. 'I've always wanted to learn, but we've never stayed in one place long enough to.'

'Oh. Right.' Ellie perked up a little. If the Andersons moved around a lot, maybe they wouldn't stay here long, either!

'Maybe you can teach me some day?'

Ellie blinked in surprise. Were all Australians this forward? 'Maybe ...' she said, but she didn't see how. Not when most of Blake's time would be spent keeping his crazy dog under control.

'Hey, did you see that?' Blake asked suddenly, gripping Choccy more tightly as the dog started to wriggle again.

'See what?'

'A mouse.'

'Don't be ridiculous! A mouse in a house full of cats?'

'I saw it. So did Choccy.'

'Nonsense.'

'Look, I'll show you where it went. You can set your cat on it.'

'Mozart's too old to chase mice.' Ellie placed the plump Persian carefully back on the piano. 'Show me.'

Mice in the building would be bad news. Ellie was pretty sure that

customers wouldn't pay to sit in a room full of rodents the way they would a room full of cats.

Still clutching Choccy tightly, Blake pushed open the storage room door. 'It wedged itself through this gap and – ah!'

Ellie followed him inside, fully expecting the mouse – if there had been a mouse – to have disappeared. Instead, there it was: a small, brown-grey mouse with big eyes and ears and a pointy nose. When it saw the children, it didn't turn and run away like a mouse should. Instead, it stood in front of the cupboard door and reared up

on its back legs. It chittered at them
angrily, boxing its paws in the air as
if scolding them.

'Bold little fellow, aren't you?'
Blake said. 'You're kind of cute.'

Ellie waved her hands at the mouse. 'Shoo! Go away.' It refused to budge.

'Maybe it's got a nest in the cupboard and it's guarding it,' Blake suggested.

'I hope not. Mum will go ballistic if we're infested.'

Ellie reached over and opened the cupboard door. The chittering grew even louder, but she couldn't see any sign of a nest. Just the mysterious trunk covered in old blankets.

'Hey, what's this?' Blake nudged the blankets off with his shoe. 'Wow, a treasure chest!' Ignoring the mouse, he knelt down to examine it.

'It's probably full of junk,' Ellie warned.

Choccy snapped his jaws at the mouse, which finally scurried away. The puppy took off after it, nosing along the skirting boards and whimpering.

'Let's open it and see,' Blake said, rattling the padlock. 'Where's the key?'

'How would I know? The trunk was already here when we moved in. The key was probably lost ages ago.'

'Maybe we can pick the lock. Have you got a bobby pin?'

Ellie shook her short brown hair.

'Hmm,' said Blake. 'If we had a hammer, we could smash it.'

'Or we could leave it alone.' Ellie fixed her cool grey eyes on Blake's sparkling blue ones. It did nothing to dampen his spirits.

'But why?' Blake said. 'It might be treasure!'

'It might not,' Ellie shot back.

'Maybe we can saw through the – No, Choccy, not now.'

The puppy kept pressing his nose into Blake's side. His mouth was moving.

'Have you picked something up again? Drop it.' Blake released the padlock and tried to pry open his dog's jaws. 'Mum says they're just like babies – always putting

things in their mouths. Very.
Strong. Babies,' he added as they
continued to tussle.

Choccy shook his head and
pulled away. It was probably an
old pen lid, Ellie thought. Typical
of a dog to eat rubbish.

'Drop it,' Blake repeated, his
voice firm.

With an apologetic tail wag,
Choccy dropped the object on
the floor.

Blake took a sharp breath, then
burst into applause. 'Good boy,
Choccy! Aren't you a clever dog!'

Ellie didn't see what was so clever
about a puppy nearly choking on

litter. Then she gasped when she saw
what Blake was looking at.

Lying on the floor,
covered in dog slobber,
was a rusty old key.

# Chapter Four

Ellie stared at the key. Could it really belong to the trunk?

'Brilliant!' Blake said, sizing up the padlock. 'It looks like it'll fit.'

'Maybe,' Ellie said, 'but it could be any old key. It might be from a door.'

'There's only one way to find out.' Blake sat back on his heels and looked meaningfully at Ellie.

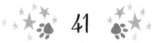

Ellie looked blankly back.

'What?' she said.

'It's your house. Your trunk. You should open it.'

'I'm not touching that!' Ellie eyed the dog drool on the key and shuddered.

Blake grinned. 'I'll do it if you like.'

Ellie wasn't sure what to do. It could be the wrong key, in which case they were wasting their time. Or maybe it was the right key, and the trunk was full of rubbish. Or maybe it was the right key, and the trunk had something dangerous in it. If not, why bother to lock it away and cover it up like that?

'All right then,' Blake continued, as if Ellie had agreed with him.

Before she could stop him, he picked up the key and inserted it in the padlock. It wouldn't turn.

'I told you. It's the wrong key.' Ellie didn't know whether to feel disappointed or relieved.

'Give me a sec.' Blake tried again. 'It's all rusty and stiff. But I think ... if I jiggle it ...' With a sharp *crack*, the padlock sprang open. 'I did it!' Blake cried.

Ellie couldn't help feeling a bit nervous. 'I don't think we should be doing this. Shouldn't we help your parents with the furniture and stuff?'

'Don't be silly. We'd just get in their way.' Blake looked at her curiously.

'Why don't you want to see inside?
Are you scared?'

'Of course not!'

Ellie squared her shoulders, then
reached over and removed the
padlock. She heaved the lid upwards
and it opened with a creak. Choccy
immediately thrust his nose inside.
Blake had to pull him away.

'What is it?' he asked impatiently as Ellie peered inside. 'Is it treasure?'

'I was right the first time,' Ellie snorted. 'It's junk.'

'What sort of junk? Let me see.'

Ellie moved out of the way so that Blake could see the trunk's contents. Much good it would do him. The trunk was full of strange things: long metal cylinders, bendy rubber tubes, yellowed bandages and empty glass bottles.

'Oh.' Blake sat back, disappointed. 'It looks like old medical equipment. A doctor's kit, maybe?'

'My great-grandfather was a vet,' Ellie said. 'This used to be his house,

 45

and he ran his practice here. It must have been his.'

'Why would he lock up his equipment and hide it?'

'Mum told me there were rumours that he was, uh –' Ellie tapped the side of her head '– not quite right. Everyone said he was a very good vet, but for some reason he went a bit weird.'

'In what way?'

Ellie shrugged. 'Mum didn't say.'

'Oh well. Treasure would have been good, but this is still interesting.' Blake reached into the trunk and pulled out something that looked like a cross between a pair of scissors and a nutcracker. 'I wonder what this is for?'

Ellie shuddered. She didn't know and she didn't want to know.

'There's heaps of cool stuff in here,' Blake said, digging around. 'Hey, what's this?' He pulled out something big, black and chunky. 'Look, a phone! I wonder how you use it?'

The phone was the old-fashioned type, with a hand-held receiver and a dial.

There were no buttons to press. Instead, there was a metal disc with a round piece of grubby paper stuck in the centre. Holes cut around the edge of the disc had numbers written inside. Ellie pressed the numbers. Nothing happened.

'Let me try.'

Blake placed a finger inside one of the holes and twisted the disc. He took his finger out and it spun noisily back into place. They looked at the phone expectantly.

'It might help if you picked the receiver up first,' said an amused voice behind them.

The children jumped. They'd been so engrossed in the old phone that they

hadn't heard Ellie's mum come up behind them.

'Shame the cord's broken. I love Bakelite phones. Was it in there?' Mum glanced inside the trunk. 'Put all that away for now,' she said, pointing at the veterinary equipment. 'But leave the phone out, I might use it as decoration for the café.'

The children re-filled the trunk and covered it with the blankets.

'Blake, your parents want you upstairs,' Mum went on. 'They want to know where you'd like your bed.'

'No worries.' Blake scrambled to his feet and picked up Choccy. 'See ya later,' he said to Ellie with a grin.

'I've got to find out what time the painters are coming. Don't forget you still haven't done your piano practice today.' Humming a tune, Mum turned and walked out of the room, leaving Ellie on her own.

Ellie groaned. She wasn't in the mood to do scales. Besides, something about the old phone fascinated her. Ellie wondered what it would have been like to live in the old days, before mobile phones and computers. This phone was so different from modern ones, it was hard to believe that people ever used it. What had Mum said? You need to pick up the receiver first?

That must be the big handle thing on top, Ellie decided. She picked it up and held it to her ear. 'Hello?' Her voice was greeted by silence. Not that she expected a reply, of course. She idly placed a finger in the dial and twisted. It spun back. This was kind of fun.

If only it still worked.

Ellie examined the electric cord that dangled off the phone's base. Mum was right; it was frayed and broken. The end was covered with tiny teeth marks, as if something had chewed through it.

As if conjured by her thoughts, the little brown-grey mouse they'd seen

earlier reappeared. It ran straight up to her, its whiskers twitching. Ellie waved the receiver to shoo it away, but that just made it bolder. With an angry squeak, it leapt onto her arm and scurried towards her face.

# Chapter Five

'Yaah!' Ellie shrieked as the mouse's stringy tail brushed against her skin. She thrashed her arms about and sprang to her feet, dropping the telephone receiver. 'Get off me!'

The mouse fell to the ground. It landed with a squeak, then pulled itself onto its hind legs. It rubbed a paw against its side and flashed Ellie an annoyed look.

'Sorry,' she found herself saying. 'But you shouldn't have climbed up on me. You gave me a fright.' She wasn't usually scared of mice. Then again, they didn't usually treat her like a ladder.

The mouse squeaked angrily.

'If you come near me again, I'll set the cats on you,' Ellie said, stamping her foot to scare the mouse away. 'Now shoo!'

The mouse retreated to a safe distance but didn't leave the room. Ellie picked up the telephone and placed it on a shelf so it wouldn't get damaged further. She was about to head to the piano when she paused.

'A few more minutes,' she murmured, 'and then I'll practise my scales.'

Ignoring the mouse's continuing scolding, Ellie dialled a few numbers at random. There was something satisfying about the *spiiiiin click-click-click* of the old phone. She tried Mum's mobile number – which took ages – and was glad that phones these days weren't such hard work. Next Ellie dialled her birthday, then the combination of her old school locker. What next? She looked at the paper in the centre of the disc. On it were numbers written in faded ink. She dialled those and–

'I must insist!' a squeaky voice said.

Ellie stared at the receiver in disbelief. Could she really hear a

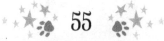

voice coming through it? Gripping it harder, she held it up to her ear. 'Um, hello?'

'Really! This is unacceptable!' the voice said.

Ellie blinked. '... Hello?'

'Is that all you can say? Can't you answer a simple question? I said:

who gave you the right to touch things that don't belong to you?'

Ellie slowly put the receiver down. The voice wasn't coming through the phone. It was behind her, near the ground. Heart thudding, Ellie turned and looked down. There was nobody there ... except for the mouse.

'Finally, you have the courtesy to look at me!'

Ellie's jaw dropped. This couldn't be happening! 'Y-you can't …' she stammered.

'Can't what?' The mouse folded its tiny paws across its chest. 'Don't tell me what I can and can't do! The cheek! First you break into my house, then you touch my things, then you hurl me to the ground–'

'Wait a minute … Your house? This is *my* house.'

'It most certainly is not.'

'Is too!' Ellie snapped back, then shook her head. She was arguing with a mouse!

'What is your name?' the mouse demanded.

Ellie didn't reply. She looked around. Was Blake hiding somewhere, playing a silly joke on her? She crossed to the door and flung it open. There was nobody there.

'If you don't tell me who you are,' the mouse continued, following her, 'I'll run up your leg!'

'I'm Ellie,' she said, squinting at the mouse. It certainly looked as if it were speaking ...

'Pardon?' The mouse crept closer, a hopeful look on its face. 'Did you by chance mean to say Elliot?'

'Of course not. I know my own name.

 59

Who's Elliot?'

'That's none of your concern. Will you leave my house quietly, or do I need to take steps to remove you?'

Ellie didn't want to think about how a mouse might go about 'removing' someone. 'And who do you think *you* are?' she asked.

'My name is Herriot,' the mouse said importantly, stroking his whiskers. 'I am the caretaker here. Just as my father was before me, and his father before him, and his father's father, and his father's father's father, and-'

'Okay, okay, I get the picture,' Ellie interrupted, holding up her hands. 'Listen, maybe you used to live here, but you can't any longer. We're here now, and you'll ruin my mum's business. Are there more of you?'

'Naturally. All of my children are here. And their children, and their children's children – there are dozens of us.'

'Dozens! Well I'm sorry, but you'll have to go–'

*'Now!'* a voice cried from the doorway.

Ellie spun around as Beethoven pounced into the centre of the room. The skinny ginger cat reached out a paw and batted at the startled mouse, which scurried away as fast as it could.

'Good boy!' Ellie cheered. She scooped up her pet and gave him a cuddle. 'You keep that nasty talking mouse away, all right?' Only now that Herriot was gone, and Ellie could hear just how silly 'talking mouse' sounded, she began to doubt what had happened.

'Mice don't talk,' she reminded

herself. 'No more than ...' Ellie looked at Beethoven; Beethoven looked at Ellie.

Ellie frowned. 'A few seconds ago, it sounded like you said "now", but you said "meow", right?'

Beethoven gave a slow blink.

'Wrong.'

# Chapter Six

Ellie let go of Beethoven with a yelp. The cat dropped to the floor, landing lightly on his feet. He twitched his tale with irritation.

'Rrreally, that was uncalled for. You've messed up my lovely coat.' Beethoven licked his fur vigorously to smooth it back down.

'You can speak too!'

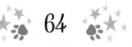

'Naturally.' Beethoven paused in his licking. 'And much better than that pesky mouse. All animals can speak. It's not our fault humans don't know how to listen.'

'But how?' Ellie gasped. 'I mean, why can I suddenly understand you?'

'How would I know?' Beethoven said, wetting a paw and using it to wash behind his ears.

'Something must have changed,' said Ellie, trying to think logically. 'I couldn't understand you earlier today, so it must have happened since then. Maybe when the Anderson's moved in?' Ellie shook her head. There was no way Blake had some magical ability to help people around him understand

animals. What else had happened? They'd chased Choccy, spotted Herriot, found the- *'That's it!'*

Just then, Blake entered the room. 'Here you are,' he said. 'Don't worry, Choccy's in the backyard.'

'That's a relief,' Beethoven said. 'That brat has no manners. And he smells like he's been rolling in his own poo.'

'Ssshh!' Ellie hissed. 'He might hear you.'

Blake raised his eyebrows. 'You mean Choccy? I told you, he's outside.'

'I wasn't speaking to you. I was ...' She stopped.

'Go on.' Beethoven's green eyes glowed with mischief. 'Tell the

puppy-chaser you can talk to cats, and that his dog stinks.'

'Ssshh!' Ellie warned again, although it was clear by now that Blake hadn't heard a word the cat said. In fact, he was looking utterly baffled.

'I didn't say anything,' he said. 'Are you sure you're all right?'

Ellie shook her head. 'You wouldn't believe me.'

'Try me.'

'It's just that I think I ... Well, I know I ...' Ellie's voice trailed off.

'Go on,' Beethoven said. 'Tell him.'

'What's wrong?' Blake looked so concerned, Ellie felt that maybe she could trust him.

'I-can-talk-to-animals.' The words came out all in one breath.

'Riiight,' Blake said, looking from Ellie to the cat and then back again. 'Meaning?'

'To Beethoven, yes. And that mouse we saw. He said he's the caretaker of this building and he wants us all to leave.' Ellie glanced at Blake uncertainly. 'Do ... do you believe me?'

'Sure.'

'Really?'

'No!' Blake's sunny blue eyes had turned stormy. 'You're just trying to get rid of us, and you think some story about a mouse is going to do the trick. Sorry, but I'm not that stupid.'

'No, I–'

'I got the feeling you didn't want us around. Is it because of Choccy?'

'No. I mean yes. I mean ... Look, maybe you can hear them too if you

concentrate,' Ellie said eagerly. 'And Beethoven, you try speaking directly to Blake.'

'Meow.'

Ellie frowned at her cat. 'Don't just say "meow"! Speak properly.'

With a satisfied look on his face, Beethoven went back to his grooming.

'Fine.' The hurt in Blake's voice was clear. 'You can't make us leave, but we don't have to be friends if you don't want to. I'll do my best to keep out of your way.'

Ellie felt a pang of guilt as he turned to walk away. It was true that she hadn't wanted another family to move in to the second flat, but she didn't want to hurt Blake's feelings, either. He actually wasn't too bad – for a boy.

Ellie grabbed his forearm. 'You're wrong! I really can talk to animals. I can prove it. I think ...'

Blake shrugged.

She dragged him towards the Bakelite telephone. 'Here,' she said, pressing the receiver into his hand. 'Dial some numbers.'

With a doubtful look, Blake dialled a few numbers. *Spiiiiiin click-click-click. Spiiiiiin click-click-click.*

'All right, Beethoven, now speak,' Ellie ordered. 'And you'd better do it properly this time.'

'Okay.' The cat stretched its back. 'What do you want me to say?'

'There!' Ellie shouted triumphantly. 'Did you hear that?'

Blake stared at her, unimpressed. 'Yeah. He's purring.'

'You're kidding!'

'No, *you're* kidding. Did you really think I'd fall for it?'

'Wait a minute. Let me think.' Ellie reached out and brushed the phone with her fingers. 'I was playing with the dial, but it didn't work straight away. Maybe it takes time or ... or it depends on the numbers ... I rang Mum's mobile, and my birthday, but ...' Ellie looked at the paper in the centre of the disc, 'it was after I dialled *these* numbers that it worked.'

'Are you saying they're magical?'

'I don't know! Just try them,' she urged.

Blake pulled a face, then dialled the faded numbers. He looked at Ellie. 'How long does it take?'

'Wait and see, you nincompoop-scoop.'

'That's not very nice,' Ellie and Blake said in unison, glaring at Beethoven.

'Hey!' Blake cried, his eyes widening as what had just happened sank in. 'We can talk to animals!'

## Chapter Seven

'I told you!' Ellie was relieved that Blake could understand what her cat was saying too. 'That proves it. It must be the phone. But how?'

Blake shrugged. 'Does it matter? We can talk to animals! I can't wait to talk to Choccy! I wonder what he'll say?'

'He *should* tell you to replace him with a cat.'

'Beethoven!' Ellie scolded. 'If you can't say something nice, don't say anything at all.'

'Fine,' the cat sniffed. 'If that's the way you want to be, I'm leaving.' And he stalked out of the room with his head held high.

Blake wasn't the least bit offended by Beethoven's bad manners – he was too excited to even care. 'I'm going to go find Choccy!' he cried as he dashed outside. Ellie followed.

Left to grow wild for years, the garden was full of waist-high weeds, unkempt bushes and overturned pieces of rusting outdoor furniture.

There was even a dirty animal hutch and a big abandoned birdcage. Tidying the garden was on Mum's to-do list. She liked the idea of an outdoor seating area – but only after the café was fully fitted out.

'Choccy!' Blake called. 'Where are you? Come here.'

The Labrador puppy exploded out of a bush. His ears flapped up and down as he ran. 'Here I am, here I am!' Choccy panted.

'Yes! You can talk too! Who's a good boy?' Blake squatted and held out his arms. He looked as excited as his puppy. 'I am, I am! Me, me, me!'

Ellie couldn't help smiling. Dogs weren't as dignified as cats, and they seemed to have a more limited vocabulary, but she had to admit that Choccy was cute. He had rolled onto his back and she was about to join Blake in tickling his tummy when a scream pierced the air.

Blake froze. 'What was that?'

'It sounded like my mum!' Without another word, they hurried back into the house, Choccy tagging eagerly along.

'Mum, what's wrong?' Ellie gasped as she ran inside.

Her mum was standing in the centre of the space that would become the cat café. She was holding her dress up above her ankles and looking at her nice new wooden counter as if she'd quite like to leap up onto it.

'Mice!' Mum shuddered. 'I saw one, but it ran away.'

Mr and Mrs Anderson had also rushed into the room to see what was going on.

'It's okay,' Mrs Anderson said soothingly. 'It's much more frightened of you than you are of it.'

Ellie wasn't so sure about that. Not if Herriot the caretaker mouse was anything to go by.

'I'm not frightened.' Blushing, Mum let her dress drape back down in soft folds. 'I just don't want the mice to scare my customers away, that's all.'

'You don't know the half of it,' Ellie murmured, casting a nervous eye around for Herriot.

'What was that?'

'Err, nothing.'

'Can I play with mice? Can I, huh, can I?' Choccy bounced about with

excitement, seeming to get under everybody's feet at once.

Ellie and Blake flashed each other a look. What if the magic had somehow spread to the grown-ups? It didn't seem as if it had, though, because they kept on talking calmly, as if the puppy hadn't spoken in perfectly clear English. It seemed that the magic only worked for people who'd used the phone and dialled the right numbers.

'I'll have to set some mouse traps,' Mum was saying. 'I've got some somewhere.'

Ellie jumped. 'What?'

'What sort have you got?' Mr Anderson asked.

'The usual. There's a spring that goes snap.'

'No need for that.' Mr Anderson shook his head. 'I can get some humane traps tomorrow.'

'What are humane traps?' Ellie asked.

'They're cruelty-free. The mouse gets lured into a box and can't get out. Then you take it away and release it.'

'That might work for one mouse,' Mum said, 'but what if there are many? And what if they come back after they're released?'

'It's worth a try at least,' Mr Anderson said.

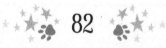

Mum didn't look convinced.

'Anyway,' Mrs Anderson said, taking her husband by the elbow. 'We'd better get back to our unpacking. We've barely started! Let us know if you need anything.'

The Andersons withdrew, but Blake stayed behind. 'I'll help Dad set the humane traps tomorrow, Mrs Walsh.'

Mum smiled weakly. 'Your father's kind to all creatures, Blake, but I've got a business to run. I can't do it if we have rats.'

'Mice,' Ellie corrected.

'What difference does it make? We'll be shut down before we even open.'

'I know, but can't we try the humane traps first?'

'No, Ellie. This is our livelihood. The sooner this is sorted, the better.'

'But Dad said-' Blake tried.

'I know what he said, but this is my house.' Ellie's mum was firm. 'I'll go get the traps. We'll start laying them down here.'

She returned with a box and a jar of peanut butter.

'What's the peanut butter for?' Ellie asked.

'Bait.'

'I thought mice ate cheese,' Blake said.

'They do, but I've read that they prefer peanut butter.'

 84

'So do I,' Ellie said in a small voice, thinking that any creature who liked peanut butter couldn't be all that bad.

'Don't *fuss*, Ellie,' Mum said. 'Mice don't have feelings the way we do.'

*Yes, they do*, Ellie thought.

'I don't like this,' she said a little later, when Mum had left the room to lay the rest of the traps upstairs. 'It doesn't feel right, not after I've spoken to Herriot. It makes the mice seem, I don't know, *human*.'

'I'm not sure what we can do,' Blake said, licking peanut butter off his fingers.

Ellie's mum had roped them both into baiting some of the traps, but

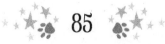

they'd drawn the line at setting
any. All the while, Blake had kept
flashing excited looks at Ellie and
winking. It wasn't that he didn't
care about the mice, but he hadn't
spoken to Herriot like she had. He
was just thrilled about being able
to talk to animals, and to Choccy
in particular.

Ellie was too, but nevertheless,
she felt subdued. She found it hard
to sleep that night. She lay awake
for hours, tossing and turning,
straining for the slightest sound
of scampering feet. Everything
was quiet. All she could do was
hope that once the mice saw the

traps, they would leave the house voluntarily.

But having met Herriot, she didn't think it was likely.

# Chapter Eight

Something made Ellie snap awake. It was a distant popping sound, like someone clicking their fingers. She opened her eyes and stared into the darkness, wondering whether the strange sound would be repeated. It wasn't.

Thinking she must have imagined it, Ellie rolled over and tried to

get back to sleep. Just as she was starting to drift off, she heard another noise. Unlike the first, this one didn't end abruptly. It continued, soft and high-pitched. After a few minutes of clutching the bedsheets and wondering what it could be, Ellie decided to investigate. Barefoot, she padded out of her bedroom and into the hallway. She walked quietly so as not to wake her mum. She listened.

The noise was a bit louder, but not much. It didn't seem to be coming from anywhere in the flat. She crept towards the front door. It grew clearer. It sounded like a voice.

Ellie eased the door open and the sound grew louder. She stepped out onto the landing. It was pitch black. Somewhere off to her left was the stairway leading up to Blake's flat and down to the ground floor. Ellie didn't want to tumble down them. Holding her hands out in front of her, she inched forwards.

'Please help me, pleeease!' the tiny voice was saying. 'It hurts!'

'I'll help you,' Ellie whispered. 'Who are you? Where are you?' She groped around for the light switch, wishing that the building wasn't still so unfamiliar.

Suddenly, a circle of bright light hit her directly in the face. Reeling backwards, she shielded her eyes with her hands and bit back a yelp of surprise.

'Oops, sorry!'

The circle of light slid down, and then she could see again. Blake was standing on the staircase, his torch pointing down towards her feet. He was dressed in striped blue pyjamas, and his hair looked more tousled than ever. Choccy was tucked under his arm.

Ellie rubbed her eyes. 'You nearly gave me a heart attack,' she muttered. 'Couldn't you give me some warning?'

 91

'Sorry,' he repeated, joining her. 'I didn't mean to scare you. I was taking Choccy out to go to the toilet. What are you doing here?'

'I heard a noise.'

'What sort of a noise?'

'Sssh. I can't hear it anymore.'

Both children held their breath and listened.

'I don't hear anything,' Blake said.

'No. Wait.' Ellie held up a hand. She heard a whimpering sound. 'It's coming from there,' she whispered, pointing to the source of the sound.

Blake aimed the torch at the wall, tracing a line along the skirting

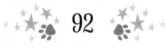

board. He stopped when the beam of light picked out a tiny figure.

It was a little mouse, even smaller than Herriot. Its paws were trembling, and its whiskers quivered. It blinked and tried to run away from the light – but it couldn't get far.

Ellie realised that the mouse was stuck fast in one of the traps Mum had laid. It was caught by its tail, and try as it might, it couldn't pull itself free.

Whimpering, Choccy tried to leap out of Blake's arms.

'Choccy,' Blake said, tightening his grip. 'Promise you'll leave the mouse alone, and I'll let you down.'

'No play?' Choccy's ears drooped

with disappointment. 'Okay.
I promise. Am good boy.'

'It's easier now that we can both
understand each other,' Blake said as
he lowered the dog to the floor. With
a sigh, Choccy rested his head on his
paws and lay obediently still.

Ellie squatted down and reached
towards the mouse. 'Don't be scared,'
she coaxed as it flinched away. 'We'll
soon get you out-'

'Ah-hah!'

Just as Ellie was about to release
the trap, a bigger mouse leapt out of
the darkness. It jumped onto her hand
and bared its sharp
front teeth at her.

'Aargh!' Shrieking, Ellie lurched backwards, shaking the mouse off.

'Sssh! Do you want to wake everyone?' Blake scolded her. 'It's only a little mouse.'

'With great big teeth!' Ellie shuddered.

'Why didn't you bite her?' A high-pitched voice came out of the darkness. 'It's no more than she deserves.'

'I missed. I'll try again.'

'Again, again, try again!'

All at once, the corridor was filled the chattering of tiny voices. Blake shone his torch on the floor and the children reeled when they saw dozens of mice. Their noses twitched and their eyes glowed eerily in the torchlight.

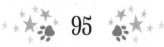

Choccy let out a low growl. Ellie backed away.

'Blake? Are you there?' A voice floated down from upstairs. 'What's going on?'

'Let me handle this,' Blake whispered to Ellie. 'Nothing, Mum! Just taking Choccy outside,' he called out, shining his torch up the stairs.

'I thought I heard you talking,' Mrs Anderson continued.

'Only to Choccy,' Blake said cheerily. 'I'll be up soon.'

Ellie heard a switch flick, and the stairway was flooded with light.

'At least see where you're going.' Mrs Anderson's shadow fell briefly

over the landing, then disappeared as she returned to their flat.

'Shouldn't we have asked her for help?' Ellie hissed, shaking a foot at the rodents.

Blake flicked off his torch. 'They're only mice. We can handle them.'

'Are you sure?'

'Of course ... And, well, I don't want Dad to know about the traps.'

'Oh ho,' the big mouse growled, 'so *you* set them.' Rearing on its back legs, it looked at the other mice and raised a paw. 'Attaaaack!'

# Chapter Nine

'Stop!' Ellie yelped, pressing back against the wall. 'We can help you! We didn't set the traps!

'Liar!' yelled a mouse with a torn ear. 'Your scent's all over them!'

'That's because we ... we *touched* them,' Ellie admitted. 'But it was wrong, and we knew it. We're sorry.'

The mice eyed her with suspicion and muttered among themselves.

'Let me near that mouse and I'll release it.'

'It?' said the big mouse again. 'How dare you call my baby girl "it"!'

'I'm sorry! Look, I can get her out, okay? Step back,' she added, not keen to feel the tough little paws on her arm again. The mice paused in their approach, but they did not retreat.

'Can we trust them?' one mouse asked another.

'What does Herriot think?' came the reply.

At the sound
of his name,
the caretaker
mouse separated
himself from the
rest of his family.
He raised himself
on his back legs and
folded his  paws across his chest.

'I knew you would be trouble,'
Herriot said, staring at the
children. 'No doubt about it,
you will have to go.'

'You can't make us,' Blake said.

'Is that so?' Herriot signalled to
the other mice, who immediately
continued creeping towards them.

'Stay back! I don't want to hurt you.' Blake shook a pyjama-clad leg at the mice. It didn't stop them. 'Ellie, get behind me. Ellie?'

But Ellie didn't reply. She was taking advantage of the distraction. Kneeling down, she reached towards the mouse trap – checked left and right to make sure that nothing was about to leap onto her – then gently and carefully eased the trap open.

*SNAP!*

It cracked shut again, and Ellie only just managed to get her fingers away in time.

The mice stopped in their tracks.

'Daddy, I'm free! And my tail's

okay, look!' The baby mouse flung herself at the mouse that had jumped on Ellie's arm. Her tail looked a bit crooked but otherwise okay. 'Please don't hurt the humans, they're *nice*. That one let me out.'

Eyes glistening, the father mouse buried his snout in his daughter's fur. He snuffled softly but did not speak.

'We really don't want to hurt you,' Ellie told the mice.

'You could have fooled me.' Herriot glanced meaningfully at the trap, but the anger had left his voice.

'It's just that we can't have you ruining the café,' Ellie added. 'People won't come here if-'

A flurry of tiny voices immediately drowned her out.

'What did she say?'

'A café? I think she said a café!'

'Oh, I love cafés!'

'Lots of table legs to climb up.'

'Think of the crumbs!'

'The crumbs, the crumbs!'

The mice chattered among themselves, excitement replacing anger.

Ellie had an idea. 'Look, how about we make a deal?'

Herriot hesitated before speaking. 'What sort of deal are you proposing?'

'Keep out of sight,' Ellie said, her words tumbling over each other in her eagerness to find a solution.

'Only come out at night when no one can see you. You can have as many café crumbs as you like, as long as you don't frighten customers away.'

'What about the traps?' the father mouse asked, one paw still wrapped protectively around his daughter.

'We'll take them away,' Ellie replied. 'If Mum doesn't see another mouse, the whole thing will soon be forgotten.'

The mice looked at each other and nodded.

'That sounds reasonable,' the father mouse said. 'I think we can do a deal.'

'Hooray, hooray! Cake crumbs every day!' The mice clung to each other and danced around in a circle, kicking up their paws in delight.

'Excuse me. Aren't we forgetting something?' Herriot's stern voice cut through the celebrations. 'I am the

caretaker here, and it is my solemn duty to protect this house from human infestation.'

The dancing stopped. The mice looked deflated.

'They admitted they were wrong,' a bold mouse ventured to say. 'I vote we let them stay.'

'Let them stay, let them stay!' a chorus of tiny voices chanted.

'Enough!' Herriot snapped. 'We await the return of The One. How can we welcome him back into our home if it's occupied?'

'The who?'

Herriot ignored Ellie's question. 'However,' he continued, 'I am prepared

to give these humans a trial run.' He held up a front paw and counted off on his toes. '*If* you immediately cease all trapping activities, and *if* you agree to supply us with unlimited crumbs from your café, and *if* you agree to leave when The One returns – then you may stay for now. We will keep out of your way and you will keep out of ours.'

Ellie shrugged. She had no idea who 'The One' was, but what choice did she have?

Holding out a forefinger, she shook Herriot's paw. 'It's a deal.'

# Chapter Ten

'Did you manage to get rid of the traps?' Blake asked Ellie the next morning. They stood on the landing in front of Ellie's flat, speaking quietly.

After all the excitement of last night, the children hadn't had much sleep. Despite that, Ellie had woken early to collect the mouse traps.

She'd dreaded the thought of finding another injured mouse too much to stay in bed. Luckily there were none.

'Yes,' Ellie said. 'I nearly trapped my finger a few times, but I think I got them all. I stuck them in a plastic bag and buried them in the bottom of the bin.'

'What did you tell your mum?' Blake asked.

'Nothing. She's too busy to notice yet. With a bit of luck, she'll forget all about them.'

'And if she doesn't?' Blake persisted.

'Then I'll tell her we found a mouse in one of the traps and you threw it away. It'll be fine as long as she doesn't see another one.' Ellie crossed her fingers that it wouldn't come to that. 'Let's just hope the mice keep their side of the bargain.'

'Yeah.' Blake was thoughtful for a moment. 'Do you know what they were talking about? Herriot said they were waiting for "The One" to come back. Who or what is that?'

Ellie shrugged. 'I dunno. He also asked me if my name was Elliot.'

'Do you think Elliot is The One?'

'I guess.' Ellie pulled a face. 'Anyway, what are you doing this morning?'

'I'm going to take Choccy outside for some training. Wanna come?'

'Sure.' Ellie had nothing else to do that morning, except practise her dreaded scales.

'Great!' Blake grinned. He looked happy that Ellie was joining them. 'I'll go get–'

'Coming!' a panting voice said. 'I heard "Choccy".' The Labrador puppy bounded down the stairs, his lead gripped between his teeth.

'Good boy!' Blake patted his dog and clipped the lead to his collar. 'Let's go.'

As the children walked down the stairs and through the empty café space, Blake explained to his pet what they were about to do. 'First we'll work on "sit".'

'I sit,' Choccy said, lowering his rump to the ground. He bounced right back up again as Beethoven stalked past, tail twitching teasingly. Choccy lunged and Blake had to pull him back.

'No, Choccy. You have to stay sitting and not stand up until I tell you – even when there are distractions. Come on, we'll try it outside.'

The high street was busy as people bustled past on their way to work. A few glanced curiously at the light coming through the café's covered windows as they walked by.

'Right. Stop here. Ignore the people, okay?' Blake ordered his dog.

 113

'I try.' Choccy fixed his eyes on his owner.

'Good. Now sit.'

Choccy sat. Ellie could tell the puppy was trying very hard to ignore any distractions, including the smell of bacon from a man's breakfast roll as he strode past.

'Down.'

Choccy flopped down obediently.

'What shop's going in there, Daddy?' came an unknown voice.

Ellie saw a girl around her age pointing at the café. She was dressed in expensive-looking clothes and was pulling a small white terrier on a lead. Choccy quivered with

excitement, but, at a stern word from Blake, he kept his gaze steady.

The girl's father snorted softly. He was a tall man in a tight suit. There was something about his expression that Ellie didn't like.

'It hardly matters, Felicity,' the man said. They continued to the traffic lights and stopped. 'It's not going to be there long.'

Ellie shuffled closer to hear what they were saying.

'Why not?' his daughter asked. 'I might like it. It might be a clothes shop.'

'From what I've heard, it's going to be a coffee shop,' the man said,

pressing the traffic light button
repeatedly.

'Boring.' The girl called Felicity
gave an exaggerated yawn.

'Don't worry, it won't last long.
If the building work for Daddy's
development across the road

doesn't put them out of business, the competing cafés inside it will. Who's going to drink somewhere that looks like it could fall down around them when they could drink somewhere clean and modern?'

'And then you'll buy this place and

turn it into something else?' The girl smiled up at him.

Her father winked. 'Once it's cheap enough.'

'Maybe a toy shop?' the girl suggested as the green man flashed up.

Ellie's heart thudded in her chest watching the girl and her father cross the road towards a park on the opposite side.

'Hey.' Blake's voice made her jump. He was standing at her shoulder, puppy training forgotten, watching them walk away. 'This might not be Australia, but I know a shark when I see one.'

'He was talking about buying Mum's café!'

Blake nodded. 'After he makes sure it fails.'

Ellie couldn't let that happen. She had to find out what was going on – and stop it before it was too late!

# Shazza the Homesick Cockatoo

Worried about the future of the cat café, *Ellie* and *Blake* investigate a rumour at the local park. It's the perfect place to test their new ability to understand animals – and there's a bird who's happy to talk.

*Shazza* the cockatoo is loud, bossy and obsessed with 'numnums'. All she wants is to return to Australia. But for now she'll settle for inviting herself home with Ellie and Blake, who soon learn that getting along with animals can be just as hard as getting along with people.

Read on for a sneak peak at
at the next book in the series!

# Magic Animal Café

## Shazza
### the Homesick
### Cockatoo

*Stella Tarakson*

Illustrated by
*Fabiana Attanasio*

Sweet
Cherry

# Chapter One

'Where do you want the espresso machine?' asked a man in overalls, hefting a large box.

'On that counter, over to the left.' Ellie's mum rubbed her hands together, looking pleased. 'It's really happening,' she said. 'Soon we'll be ready to open!'

Ellie hadn't seen her mum look so happy in years. Even yesterday's

worrying news hadn't upset her. Ellie had overheard a man planning to build something across the road that would have other coffee shops inside it. They would be clean and modern, unlike Mum's café, which was on the ground floor of a tired old building. The man had gone on to say that when Mum's café flopped, he would buy it from her at a low price.

Ellie's mum had refused to be frightened. 'I'm not going to be bullied by developers,' she'd insisted. 'People will come to us because we're different - there are no other cat cafés around! Cattucino will do well, you'll see.'

Ellie was glad Mum was so confident, but wished she'd take the threat more seriously. At least she could try to find out more about it. Ellie and her new friend Blake couldn't help feeling worried.

'Why don't they have dog cafés, too?' Blake asked, holding his wriggling Labrador puppy against his chest. Blake and his parents had moved into the second floor flat above the café, while Ellie and her mum lived on the first floor. They'd moved to England from Australia to set up an animal rescue centre.

Ellie rolled her eyes at Blake's question. 'Maybe it's because people don't like getting slobbered over.'

Ellie had never been much of a dog person. Cats were calmer, quieter and neater – Ellie and her mum owned eight of them. They were all going to be part of the new café. But she had to admit that she was starting to like Choccy, who was rather sweet. She ruffled the puppy's ears and he wagged his tail.

'See, Ellie?' Choccy said, his tail thumping against Blake. 'No licking.'

'That's right. You're a fast learner–' Ellie started to say, before Blake flashed her a warning look. Ellie clamped her mouth shut. She checked to see whether

Mum had noticed, but she was busy watching the men putting the espresso machine in place.

Ellie and Blake had an agreement. For the time being at least, they weren't going to tell anybody that they could talk to animals. It was more fun to keep it to themselves.

Ellie and Blake weren't sure exactly how, but their exciting new ability had something to do with an old-fashioned telephone they'd found. The magic started just after the children rang the faded numbers written on a piece of paper in the centre of the dial.

'Scuse me, careful now.'

Something hard bumped against

Ellie's back. She stepped forward as a man carrying a rug pushed past her, straight into the path of two others who were moving a table.

'Why don't you two go out for a bit?' Mum suggested, pointing out the spot where she wanted the table placed. 'Have some fun before school starts. There's a park across the road. You could take your sketch pad and do a drawing for me.'

Ellie and Blake exchanged a look. Yesterday the man had said the new development would be across the road.

Ellie grabbed her sketching set, Blake clipped on Choccy's lead, and they were out the door.